Anna Letitia Barbauld

Hymns in Prose for Children

Anna Letitia Barbauld

Hymns in Prose for Children

ISBN/EAN: 9783744780766

Printed in Europe, USA, Canada, Australia, Japan

Cover: Foto ©Andreas Hilbeck / pixelio.de

More available books at **www.hansebooks.com**

HYMNS IN PROSE
FOR
CHILDREN.

BY MRS. BARBAULD.

AUTHOR OF "LESSONS FOR CHILDREN."

ILLUSTRATED.

NEW YORK:
HURD & HOUGHTON, 401, BROADWAY.
LONDON: JOHN MURRAY.
1866.

PREFACE.

AMONG the number of books composed for the use of children, though there are many, and some on a very rational plan, which unfold the system, and give a summary of the doctrines of religion, it would be difficult to find one calculated to assist them in the devotional part of it, except indeed Dr. Watts's Hymns for Children. These are in pretty general use ; and the author is deservedly honoured for the condescension of his Muse, which was very able to take a loftier flight. But it may well be doubted whether poetry ought to be lowered to the capacities of children, or whether they should not rather be kept from reading verse till they are able to relish good verse; for the very essence of poetry is an elevation in thought and style above the common standard ; and if it wants this character, it wants all that renders it valuable.

The author of these Hymns has therefore chosen to give them in prose. They are intended to be committed to memory, and recited. And it will probably be found that the measured prose in which such pieces

b

are generally written, is nearly as agreeable to the ear as a more regular rythmus. Many of these Hymns are composed in alternate parts, which will give them something of the spirit of social worship.

The peculiar design of this publication is to impress devotional feelings as early as possible on the infant mind ; fully convinced, as the Author is, that they cannot be impressed too soon, and that a child, to feel the full force of the idea of God, ought never to remember the time when he had no such idea — to impress them, by connecting religion with a variety of sensible objects, with all that he sees, all he hears, all that affects his young mind with wonder or delight ; and thus, by deep, strong, and permanent associations, to lay the best foundation for practical devotion in future life. For he who has early been accustomed to see the Creator in the visible appearances of all around him, to feel His continual presence, and lean upon His daily protection—though his religious ideas may be mixed with many improprieties, which his correcter reason will refine away—has made large advances towards that habitual piety, without which religion can scarcely regulate the conduct, and will never warm the heart.

A. L. B.

PREFACE TO THE PRESENT EDITION.

In offering this volume to the public, little need be said in addition to the original Preface, in which the Authoress fully explains the character and intention of the work; an effort singularly successful in raising the youthful mind to the praise of God, through the contemplation of His works.

To realise this conception more vividly than mere text can accomplish, has been the aim and intention throughout.

The varied and picturesque descriptions with which the continuous thread of argument is strung, render the task of illustration at once easy and suggestive.

Few works could be found which challenge the pencil and fancy of the artist in a greater degree; and it is hoped the present effort may be deemed worthy of the text.

The blending of the illustrations with the type will be found no unimportant feature; a unity being thereby obtained, which is alike pleasing and less fatiguing both to the mind and eye, a matter of some importance with the young.

LONDON, NOVEMBER, 1863.

LIST OF ILLUSTRATIONS.

ENGRAVED BY JAMES D. COOPER.

HYMN I.

COME, let us praise God, for He is ex-
ceeding great; let us bless God, for
He is very good.

He made all things; the sun to rule the
day, the moon to shine by night.

He made the great whale, and the elephant;
and the little worm that crawleth on the
ground.

B

The little birds sing praises to God, when they warble sweetly in the green shade.

The brooks and rivers praise God, when they murmur melodiously amongst the smooth pebbles.

I will praise God with my voice; for I may praise Him, though I am but a little child.

A few years ago, and I was a little infant, and my tongue was dumb within my mouth:

And I did not know the great name of God, for my reason was not come unto me.

But now I can speak, and my tongue shall praise Him:

I can think of all His kindness, and my heart shall love Him.

Let Him call me, and I will come unto Him: let Him command, and I will obey Him.

When I am older, I will praise Him better; and I will never forget God, so long as my life remaineth in me.

HYMN II.

Come, let us go forth into the fields, let us see how the flowers spring, let us listen to the warbling of the birds, and sport ourselves upon the new grass.

The winter is over and gone, the buds come out upon the trees, the crimson blossoms of the peach and the nectarine are seen, and the green leaves sprout.

The hedges are bordered with tufts of primroses, and yellow cowslips, that hang down their heads; and the blue violet lies hid beneath the shade.

The young goslings are running upon the green, they are just hatched, their bodies are covered with yellow down; the old ones hiss with anger if any one comes near.

The hen sits on her nest of straw, she watches patiently the full time, then she carefully breaks the shell, and the young chickens come out.

The lambs just dropped are in the field, they totter by the side of their dams, their young limbs can hardly support their weight. If you fall, little lambs, you will not be hurt; there is spread under you a carpet of soft grass; it is spread on purpose to receive you.

The butterflies flutter from bush to bush and open their wings to the warm sun.

The young animals of every kind are sporting about, they feel themselves happy, they are glad to be alive,—they thank Him that hath made them alive.

They may thank Him in their hearts, but we can thank Him with our tongues; we are better than they, and can praise Him better.

The birds can warble and the young lambs can bleat, but we can open our lips in His praise, we can speak of all His goodness.

Therefore we will thank Him for ourselves, and we will thank Him for those that cannot speak.

Trees that blossom and little lambs that skip about, if you could, you would say how good He is; but you are dumb, we will say it for you.

We will not offer you in sacrifice, but we will offer sacrifice for you; on every hill and in every green field, we will offer the sacrifice of thanksgiving, and the incense of praise.

c

HYMN III.

BEHOLD the shepherd of the flock, he taketh care for his sheep, he leadeth them among clear brooks, he guideth them to fresh pasture: if the young lambs are weary, he carrieth them in his arms; if they wander, he bringeth them back.

But who is the shepherd's Shepherd? who taketh
care for him? who guideth him in the path he should
go? and, if he wander, who shall bring him back? God
is the shepherd's Shepherd. He is the Shepherd over all;
He taketh care for all; the whole earth is His fold; we
are all His flock; and every herb, and every
green field, is the pasture
which He hath prepared
for us.

The mother loveth her little child; she bringeth it up on her knees; she nourisheth its body with food; she feedeth its mind with knowledge; if it is sick, she nurseth it with tender love; she watcheth over it when asleep; she forgetteth it not for a moment; she teacheth it how to be good; she rejoiceth daily in its growth.

But who is the Parent of the mother? who nourisheth her with good things, and watcheth over her with tender love, and remembereth her every moment? Whose arms are about her to guard her from harm? and if she is sick, who shall heal her.

God is the Parent of the mother; He is the Parent of all, for He created all. All the men and all the women, who are alive in the wide world, are His children; He loveth all, He is good to all.

The king governeth his people; he hath a golden crown upon his head, and the royal sceptre is in his hand; he sitteth upon a throne, and sendeth forth his demands; his subjects fear before him: if they do well, he protecteth them from danger; and if they do evil, he punisheth them.

But who is the Sovereign of the king? who commandeth him what he must do? whose hand is reached out to protect him from danger? and if he doeth evil, who shall punish him?

God is the Sovereign of the king; His crown is of rays of light, and His throne is amongst the stars. He is King of kings, and Lord of lords: if He biddeth us live, we live; and if He biddeth us die, we die: His dominion is over all worlds, and the light of His countenance is upon all His works.

God is our Shepherd, therefore we will
follow Him ; God is our Father, therefore we
will love Him ; God is our King, therefore
we will obey Him.

HYMN IV.

COME, and I will show you what is beautiful. It is a rose fully blown. See how she sits upon her mossy stem, like the queen of all the flowers! her leaves glow like fire: the air is filled with her sweet odour; she is the delight of every eye.

She is beautiful, but there is a fairer than she. He that made the rose is more beautiful than the rose; He is all lovely; He is the delight of every heart.

I will show you what is strong. The lion is strong; when he raiseth up himself from his lair, when he shaketh his mane, when the voice of his roaring is heard, the cattle of the field fly, and the wild beasts of the desert hide themselves, for he is very terrible.

The lion is strong, but He that made the lion is stronger than he: His anger is terrible: He could make us die in a moment, and no one could save us out of His hand.

I will show you what is glorious. The sun is glorious. When he shineth in the clear sky, when he sitteth on the bright throne in the heavens, and looketh abroad over all the earth, he is the most excellent and glorious creature the eye can behold.

The sun is glorious, but He that made the sun is more glorious than he. The eye beholdeth Him not, for His brightness is more dazzling than we could bear.

He seeth in all dark places; by night as well as by day; and the light of His countenance is over all His works.

Who is this great Name, and what is He called, that my lips may praise Him?

This great Name is GOD. He made all things, but He is himself more excellent than all which He hath made: they are beautiful, but He is beauty; they are strong, but He is strength; they are perfect, but He is perfection.

HYMN V.

THE glorious sun is set in the west ; the night dews fall ; and the air, which was sultry, becomes cool.

The flowers fold up their coloured leaves ; they fold themselves up, and hang their heads on the slender stalk.

The chickens are gathered under the wing of the hen, and are at rest ; the hen herself is at rest also.

The little birds have ceased their warbling, they are asleep on the boughs, each one has his head behind his wing.

There is no murmur of bees around the hive, or among the honeyed woodbines; they have done their work, and lie close in their waxen cells.

The sheep rest upon their soft fleeces, and their loud bleating is no more heard amongst the hills.

There is no sound of a number of voices, or of children at play, or the trampling of busy feet, and of people hurrying to and fro.

The smith's hammer is not heard upon the anvil; nor the harsh saw of the carpenter.

All men are stretched on their quiet beds; and the child sleeps upon the breast of its mother.

Darkness is spread over the skies, and darkness is upon the ground; every eye is shut and every hand is still.

Who taketh care of all people when they are sunk in sleep; when they cannot defend themselves, nor see if danger approacheth?

There is an eye that never sleepeth; there is an eye that seeth in dark night as well as in the bright sunshine.

When there is no light of the sun, nor of the moon; when there is no lamp in the house, nor any little star twinkling through the thick clouds; that eye seeth everywhere, in all places, and watcheth continually over all the families of the earth.

The eye that sleepeth not is God's; His hand is always stretched out over us.

He made sleep to refresh us when we are weary: He made night that we might sleep in quiet.

As the mother moveth about the house with her finger on her lips, and stilleth every little noise that her infant be not disturbed,—as she draweth the curtains around its bed, and shutteth out the light from its tender eyes, so God draweth the curtains of darkness around us; so He maketh all things to be hushed and still, that His large family may sleep in peace.

Labourers, spent with toil, and young children, and every little humming insect, sleep quietly, for God watcheth over you.

You may sleep, for He never sleeps; you may close your eyes in safety, for His eye is always open to protect you.

When the darkness is passed away, and the beams of the morning sun strike through your eyelids, begin the day with praising God, who hath taken care of you through the night.

Flowers, when you open again, spread your leaves, and smell sweet to His praise.

Birds, when you awake, warble your thanks amongst the green boughs; sing to Him before you sing to your mates.

Let His praise be in our hearts, when we lie down; let His praise be on our lips, when we awake.

HYMN VI.

CHILD of reason, whence comest thou? What has thine eye observed, and whither has thy foot been wandering?

I have been wandering along the meadows in the thick grass; the cattle were feeding around me, or reposing in the cool shade; the corn sprung up in the furrows;

the poppy and the harebell grew among the wheat; the fields were bright with summer, and glowing with beauty.

Didst thou see nothing more? Didst thou observe nothing besides? Return again, child of reason, for there are greater things than these.— God was among the fields; and didst thou not perceive Him? His beauty was upon the meadows: His smiles enlivened the sunshine.

I have walked through the thick fo-rest ; the wind whis-pered among the trees ; the brook fell from the rocks with a pleasant murmur ; the squirrel leapt from bough to bough ; and the birds sung to each other amongst the branches.

Didst thou hear nothing but the murmur of the brook? no whispers but the whispers of the wind? Return again, child of reason, for there are greater things than these.—God was amongst the trees; His voice sounded in the murmur of the water;

His music warbled in the shade; and didst thou not attend?

I saw the moon rising behind the trees; it was like a lamp of gold. The stars one after another appeared in the clear firmament.

Presently I saw black clouds arise, and roll towards the south; the lightning streamed in thick flashes over the sky; the thunder growled at a distance; it came nearer, and I felt afraid, for it was loud and terrible.

Did thy heart feel no terror, but of the thunderbolt? Was there nothing bright and terrible but the lightning? Return, O child of reason, for there are greater things than these.—God was in the storm, and didst thou not perceive Him?

His terrors were abroad, and did not thine heart acknowledge Him?

God is in every place; He speaks in every sound we hear; He is seen in all that our eyes behold; nothing, O child of reason, is without God;—let God therefore be in all thy thoughts.

HYMN VII.

COME, let us go into the thick shade, for it is the noon of day, and the summer sun beats hot upon our heads.

The shade is pleasant and cool; the branches meet above our heads, and shut out the sun as with a green curtain; the grass is soft to our feet, and a clear brook washes the roots of the trees.

The sloping bank is covered with flowers; let us lie down upon it; let us throw our limbs on the fresh grass and sleep; for all things are still, and we are quite alone.

The cattle can lie down to sleep in the cool shade, but we can do what is better; we can raise our voices to heaven; we can praise the great God who made us.

He made the warm sun and the cool shade; the trees that grow upwards, and the brooks that run murmuring along. All the things that we see are His work.

Can we raise our voices up to the high heaven? Can we make Him hear who is above the stars? We need not raise our voices to the stars: for He heareth us when we only whisper: when we breathe out words softly with a low voice. He that filleth the heavens is here also.

May we that are so young speak to Him that always was? May we, that can hardly speak plain, speak to God?

We that are so young are but lately made alive; therefore we should not forget His forming hand who hath made us alive. We that cannot speak plain, should lisp out praises to Him who teacheth us how to speak, and hath opened our dumb lips.

When we could not think of Him, He thought of us; before we could ask Him to bless us, He had already given us many blessings.

He fashioneth our tender limbs, and causeth them to grow; He maketh us strong, and tall, and nimble.

Every day we are more active than the former day, therefore every day we ought to praise Him better than the former day.

The buds spread into leaves, and the blossoms swell to fruit; but they know not how they grow, nor who caused them to spring up from the bosom of the earth.

Ask them if they will tell thee; bid them to break forth into singing, and fill the air with pleasant sounds.

They smell sweet; they look beautiful; but they are quite silent: no sound is in the still air; no murmur of voices amongst the green leaves.

The plants and the trees are made to give fruit to man; but man is made to praise God who made him.

We love to praise Him, because He loveth to bless us; we thank Him for life, because it is a pleasant thing to be alive.

We love God, who hath created all beings; we love all beings, because they are the creatures of God. We cannot be good, as God is good, to all persons everywhere; but we can rejoice that everywhere there is a God to do them good.

We will think of God when we play, and when we work; when we walk out, and when we come in; when we sleep, and when we wake; His praise shall dwell continually upon our lips.

HYMN VIII.

SEE where stands the cottage of the labourer covered with warm thatch! The mother is spinning at the door; the young children sport before her on the grass; the elder ones learn to labour, and are obedient; the father worketh to provide them food: either he tilleth the ground, or he gathereth in the corn, or shaketh his ripe apples from the tree. His children run to meet him when he cometh home, and his wife prepareth the wholesome meal.

The father, the mother, and the children make a family; the father is the master thereof. If the family be numerous, and the grounds large, there are servants to help to do the work: all these dwell in one house; they sleep beneath the same roof; they eat the same

bread; they kneel down together and praise God every night and every morning with one voice; they are very closely united, and are dearer to each other than any strangers. If one is sick they mourn together; and if one is happy they rejoice together.

Many houses are built together; many families live near one another; they meet together on the green, and in pleasant walks, and to buy and sell, and in the house of justice: and the sound of the bell calleth them to the house of God in company. If one is poor, his

neighbour helpeth him; if he is sad, he comforteth him. This is a village; see where it stands enclosed in a green shade, and the tall spire peeps above the trees.

If there be very many houses, it is a town, it is governed by a magistrate.

Many towns, and a large extent of country, make a kingdom; it is enclosed by mountains; it is divided by rivers; it is washed by seas; the inhabitants thereof are countrymen; they speak the same language; they

make war and peace together; a king is the ruler thereof. Many kingdoms and countries full of people, and islands, and large continents, and different climates,

make up this whole world—God governeth it. The people swarm upon the face of it like ants upon a hillock; some are black with the hot sun; some cover themselves with furs against the sharp cold ; some drink of the fruit of the vine ; some the pleasant milk of the cocoa-nut, and others quench their thirst with the running stream.

All are God's family ; He knoweth every one of them, as a shepherd knoweth his flock ; they pray to Him in different languages, but He understandeth them all ; He heareth them all ; He taketh care of all : none are so great that He cannot punish them ; none are so mean that He will not protect them.

H

Negro woman, who sittest pining in captivity, and weepest over thy sick child: though no one seeth thee, God seeth thee; though no one pitieth thee, God pitieth thee; raise thy voice, forlorn and abandoned one; call upon Him from amidst thy bonds, for assuredly He will hear thee.

Monarch, that rulest over a hundred states; whose frown is terrible as death, and whose armies cover the land, boast not thyself as though there were none above thee:—God is above thee; His powerful arm is always over thee; and if thou doest ill, assuredly He will punish thee.

Nations of the earth, fear the Lord; families of men, call upon the name of your God.

Is there any one whom God hath not made? let him not worship Him: is there any one whom He hath not blessed? let him not praise Him.

HYMN IX.

Come, let us walk abroad;
let us talk of the works of God.
Take up a handful of sand;
number the grains of it; tell them
one by one into your lap.
Try if you can count the
blades of grass in the field,
or the leaves on the trees.
You cannot count them, they are innumerable;
much more the things which God has made.

The fir groweth on the high mountain, and the grey willow bends above the stream.

The thistle is armed with
    sharp prickles,

    the mallow
        is
soft and woolly.

The hop
layeth hold with
her tendrils,
and claspeth the
tall pole;
the oak hath firm
root in the
ground,
and resisteth the
winter storm.

The daisy
enamelleth the meadows, and groweth beneath the
foot of the passenger.

The tulip
asketh a rich soil, and the careful hand of
the gardener.

The iris and the reed spring up in the marsh ; the rich grass covereth the meadows ; and the purple heath-flower enliveneth the waste ground.

The water-lilies grow beneath
the stream ; their broad leaves
float on the surface of the water;
the wall-flower takes root in the
hard stone, and spreads its fra-
grance amongst broken ruins.

Every leaf is of a different form; every plant hath a separate inhabitant.

Look at the thorns that are white with blossoms, and the flowers that cover the fields, and the plants that are trodden in the green path. The hand of man hath not planted them; the sower hath not scattered the seeds from his hand, nor the gardener digged a place for them with his spade.

Some grow on steep rocks, where no man can climb; in shaking bogs, and deep forests, and desert islands: they spring up everywhere, and cover the bosom of the whole earth.

Who causeth them to grow everywhere, and bloweth the seeds about in winds, and mixeth them with the mould, and watereth them with soft rains, and cherisheth them with dews? Who fanneth them with the pure breath of heaven; and giveth them colours and smells, and spreadeth out their thin transparent leaves?

How doth the rose draw its crimson
from the dark brown earth, or
the lily its shining white? How
can a small seed contain a plant?
How doth every plant know its
season to put forth? They are
marshalled in order: each one
knoweth his place, and standeth
up in his own rank.

The snow-drop and the prim-
rose make haste to lift their heads
above the ground. When the spring
cometh, they say, Here we are.
The carnation waiteth for the
full strength of the year; and
the hardy laurustinus cheereth the
winter months.

Every plant produceth its like.
An ear of corn will not grow
from an acorn; nor will a grape-
stone produce cherries; but every
one springeth from its proper
seed.

Who preserveth them alive through the cold winter, when the snow is on the ground, and the sharp frost bites on the plain ? Who soweth a small seed, and a little warmth in the bosom of the earth, and causeth them to spring up afresh, and sap to rise through the hard fibres ?

The trees are withered, naked and bare ; they are like dry bones.

Who breathed on them with the breath of spring,
and they are covered with verdure, and green leaves
sprout from the dead wood?

Lo, these are a part of His works;
and a little portion of His wonders.

There is little need that I
should tell you of God, for
everything speaks of Him.

Every field is like an open
book; every painted flower hath
a lesson written on its leaves.

Every murmuring brook hath
a tongue; a voice is in every
whispering wind.

K

They all speak of Him who made them; they all tell us, He is very good.

We cannot see God, for He is invisible; but we can see His works, and worship His footsteps in the green sod. They that know the most will praise God the best; but which of us can number half His works?

HYMN X.

LOOK at that spreading oak, the pride of the village green : its trunk is massy, its branches are strong. Its roots, like crooked fangs, strike deep into the soil, and support its huge bulk. The birds build among the boughs : the cattle repose beneath its shade : the neighbours form groups beneath the shelter of its green canopy. The old men point it out to their children, but they themselves remember not its growth : generations of men one after another have been born and died, and this son of the forest has remained the same, defying the storms of two hundred winters.

Yet this large tree was once a little acorn; small in size, insignificant in appearance; such as you are now picking up upon the grass beneath it. Such an acorn, whose cup can only contain a drop or two of dew, contained the whole oak. All its massy trunk, all its knotted branches, all its multitude of leaves, were in that acorn; it grew, it spread, it unfolded itself by degrees, it received nourishment from the rain, and the dews, and the well-adapted soil, but it was all there. Rain and dews, and soil, could not raise an oak without the acorn;

nor could they make the acorn any-
thing but an oak.

The mind of a child is like the
acorn; its powers are folded up, they
do not yet appear, but they are all
there. The memory, the judgment,
the invention, the feeling of right and
wrong, are all in the mind of a child;
of a little infant just born; but they
are not expanded, you cannot perceive
them.

Think of the wisest man you ever
knew or heard of; think of the greatest
man; think of the most learned man,
who speaks a number of languages
and can find out hidden things; think
of a man who stands like that tree,

sheltering and protecting a number of his fellow men, and then say to yourself, the mind of that man was once like mine, his thoughts were childish like my thoughts, nay, he was like the babe just born, which knows nothing, remembers nothing, which cannot distinguish good from evil, nor truth from falsehood.

If you had only seen an acorn, you could never guess at the form and size of an oak; if you had never conversed with a wise man, you could form no idea of him from the mute and helpless infant.

Instruction is the food of the mind; it is like the dew and the rain and the rich soil.

As the soil and the rain and the dew cause the tree to swell and put forth its tender shoots, so do books and study and discourse feed the mind, and make it unfold its hidden powers.

Reverence therefore your own mind; receive the nurture of instruction, that the man within you may grow and flourish. You cannot guess how excellent he may become.

It was long before this oak showed its greatness; year after year passed away, and it had only shot a little way above the ground, a child might have plucked it up with his little hands; it was long before any one called it a tree; it is long before the child becomes a man.

L

The acorn might have perished in the ground, the young tree might have been shorn of its graceful boughs, the twig might have bent, and the tree would have been crooked, but if it grew at all, it could have been nothing but an oak, it would not have been grass or flowers, which live their season and then perish from the face of the earth.

The child may be a foolish man, he may be a wicked man, but he must be a man; his nature is not that of any inferior creature, his soul is not akin to the beasts that perish.

O cherish then this precious mind, feed it with truth, nourish it with knowledge; it comes from God, it is made in His image: the oak will last for centuries, but the mind of man is made for immortality.

Respect in the infant the future man. Destroy not in man the rudiments of an angel.

HYMN XI.

The golden orb of the sun is sunk behind the hills, the colours fade away from the western sky, and the shades of evening fall fast around me.

Deeper and deeper they stretch over the plain; I look at the grass, it is no longer green; the flowers are no more tinted with various hues; the houses, the trees, the cattle, are all lost in the distance. The dark curtain of night is let down over the works of God ; they are blotted out from the view as if they were no longer there.

Child of little observation, canst thou see nothing because thou canst not see grass and flowers, trees and cattle ? Lift up thine eyes from the ground shaded

with darkness, to the heavens that are stretched over thy head ; see how the stars one by one appear and light up the vast concave. There is the moon bending her bright horns like a silver bow, and shedding her mild light, like liquid silver, over the blue firmament. There is Venus, the evening and morning star ; and the

Pleiades, and the Bear that never sets, and the Pole star that guides the mariner over the deep.

Now the mantle of darkness is over the earth; the last little gleam of twilight is faded away; the lights are extinguished in the cottage windows, but the firmament

burns with innumerable fires; every little star twinkles in its place. If you begin to count them they are more than you can number; they are like the sands on the sea shore. The telescope shows you far more, and there are thousands and ten thousands of stars which no telescope has ever reached.

Now Orion heaves his bright shoulder above the horizon, and Sirius, the Dog-star, follows him the brightest of the train.

Look at the milky way, it is a field of brightness; its pale light is composed of myriads of burning suns.

All these are God's families. He gave the sun to shine with a ray of His own glory; He marks the path of the planets, He guides their wanderings through the sky, and traces out their orbit with the finger of His power.

If you were to travel as swift as an arrow from a bow, and to travel on further and further still for millions of years, you would not be out of the creation of God.

New suns in the depth of space would still be burning round you, and other planets fulfilling their appointed course.

Lift up thine eyes, child of earth, for God has given thee a glimpse of heaven. The light of one sun is withdrawn that thou mayest see ten thousand. Darkness is spread over the earth that thou mayest behold, at a distance, the regions of eternal day.

This earth has a variety of inhabitants; the sea, the air, the surface of the ground, swarm with creatures of different natures, sizes, and powers; to know a very little of them is to be wise among the sons of men. What then, thinkest thou, are the various forms and natures and senses and occupations of the peopled universe?

M

Who can tell the birth and generations of so many worlds? who can relate their histories? who can describe their inhabitants?

Canst thou measure infinity with a line? canst thou grasp the circle of infinite space.

Yet all these depend upon God, they hang upon Him as a child upon the breast of its mother; He tempereth the heat to the inhabitant of Mercury; He provideth resources against the cold in the frozen orb of Saturn. Doubt not that He provideth for all beings that He has made.

Look at the moon when it walketh in brightness; gaze at the stars when they are marshalled in the firmament, and adore the Maker of so many worlds.

HYMN XII.

IT is now Winter, dead Winter. Desolation and silence reign in the fields, no singing of birds is heard, no humming of insects. The streams murmur no longer; they are locked up in frost.

The trees lift their naked boughs like withered arms into the bleak sky, the green sap no longer rises in their veins; the flowers and the sweet-smelling shrubs are decayed to their roots.

The sun himself looks cold and cheerless; he gives light only enough to show the universal desolation.

Nature, child of God, mourns
for her children. A little while
ago and she rejoiced in her off-
spring: the rose spread its per-
fume upon the gale; the vine
gave its fruit; her children were
springing and blooming around
her, on every lawn and every
green bank.

O Nature, beautiful Nature,
beloved child of God, why dost
thou sit mourning and desolate?
Has thy Father forsaken thee?
has He left thee to perish? Art
thou no longer the object of His
care?

He has not forsaken thee, O
Nature? thou art His beloved
child, the eternal image of His
perfections: His own beauty is
spread over thee, the light of
His countenance is shed upon
thee.

Thy children shall live again, they shall spring up and bloom around thee; the rose shall again breathe its sweetness on the soft air, and from the bosom of the ground verdure shall spring forth.

And dost thou not mourn, O Nature, for thy human births; for thy sons and thy daughters that sleep under the sod ; and shall not they also revive ? Shall the rose and the myrtle bloom anew, and shall man perish ? Shall goodness sleep in the ground, and the light of wisdom be quenched in the dust, and shall tears be shed over them in vain ?

They also shall live; their winter shall pass away; they shall bloom again. The tears of thy children shall be dried up when the eternal year proceeds. O come that eternal year!

CHILD of mortality, whence comest thou? why is thy countenance sad, and why are thine eyes red with weeping?

I have seen the rose in its beauty; it spread its leaves to the morning sun—I returned, it was dying upon its stalk; the grace of the form of it was gone; its loveliness was vanished away; the leaves thereof were scattered on the ground, and no one gathered them again.

A stately tree grew on the plain; its branches were covered with verdure; its boughs spread wide and made a goodly shadow; the trunk was like a strong pillar; the roots were like crooked fangs—I returned, the verdure was nipped by the east wind; the branches were lopped away by the axe; the worm had made its way into the trunk, and the heart thereof was decayed; it mouldered away, and fell to the ground.

I have seen insects sporting in the sunshine, and darting along the streams; their wings glittered with gold and purple; their bodies shone like the green emerald : they were more numerous than I could count; their motions were quicker than my eye could glance—I returned, they were brushed into the pool; they were perishing with the evening breeze; the swallow had devoured them; the pike had seized them; there were none found of so great a multitude.

I have seen a man in the pride of his strength;
his cheeks glowed with beauty; his limbs were full
of activity; he leaped; he walked; he ran; he
rejoiced in that he was more excellent than those—
I returned, he lay stiff and cold on the bare ground;
his feet could no longer move, nor his hands stretch
themselves out; his life was departed from him; and
therefore do I weep because Death is in the world;
the spoiler is among the works of God: all that is
made must be destroyed; all that is born must die:
let me alone, for I will weep yet longer.

HYMN XIV

I HAVE seen the flower withering on the stalk, and its bright leaves spread on the ground—I looked again, and it sprung forth afresh; the stem was crowned with new buds, and the sweetness thereof filled the air.

I have seen the sun set in the west, and the shades of night shut in the wide horizon; there was no colour, nor shape, nor beauty, nor music; gloom and darkness brooded around—I looked, the sun broke forth again from the east, he gilded the mountain tops; the lark rose to meet him from her low nest, and the shades of darkness fled away.

I have seen the insect, being come to its full size, languish and refuse to eat: it spun itself a tomb, and was shrouded in the silken cone; it lay without feet, or shape, or power to move. I looked again, it had burst its tomb: it was full of life, and sailed on coloured wings through the soft air; it rejoiced in its new being.

Thus shall it be with thee, O man! and so shall thy life be renewed.

Beauty shall spring up out of ashes; and life out of the dust.

A little while thou shalt lie in the ground, as the seed lieth in the bosom of the earth; but thou shalt be raised again; and if thou art good thou shalt never die any more.

Who is He that cometh to burst open the prison doors of the tomb, to bid the dead awake, and to gather His redeemed from the four winds of heaven?

He descendeth on a fiery cloud; the sound of a trumpet goeth before Him; thousands of angels are on His right hand.

It is JESUS, the Son of God; the Saviour of men; the friend of the good.

He cometh in the glory of His Father; He hath received power from on high.

Mourn not, therefore, child of mortality;—for the spoiler, the cruel spoiler, that laid waste the works of God is subdued; JESUS hath conquered death: child of immortality! mourn no longer.

HYMN XV.

THE rose is sweet, but it is surrounded with thorns; the lily of the valley is fragrant, but it springeth up amongst the brambles. The spring is pleasant, but it is soon past: the summer is bright, but the winter destroyeth the beauty thereof.

The rainbow is very glorious,
but it soon vanisheth away: life is good, but it is
quickly swallowed up in death.

There is a land where the roses are without thorns, where the flowers are not mixed with brambles.

In that land there is eternal spring, and light without any cloud.

The tree of life groweth in the midst thereof ; rivers of pleasures are there, and flowers that never fade.

Myriads of happy spirits are there, and surround the throne of God with a perpetual hymn.

The angels with their golden harps sing praises continually, and the cherubim fly on wings of fire.

This country is Heaven : it is the country of those that are good ; and nothing that is wicked must enter there.

The toad must not spit its venom amongst turtle doves; nor the poisonous henbane grow amongst sweet flowers. Neither must any one that doeth ill enter into that good land.

This earth is pleasant, for it is God's earth, and it is filled with many delightful things.

But that country is far better; there we shall not grieve any more, nor be sick any more, nor do wrong any more; there the cold of winter shall not wither us, nor the heats of summer scorch us.

In that country there are no wars nor quarrels, but all love one another with dear love.

When our parents and friends die, and are laid in the cold ground, we see them here no more; but there we shall embrace them again, and live with them and be separated no more.

There we shall meet all good men, whom we read of in holy books. There we shall see Abraham, the called of God, the father of the faithful; and Moses, after his long wanderings in the Arabian desert; and Elijah, the prophet of God; and Daniel, who escaped from the lions' den; and there the son of Jesse, the shepherd king, the sweet singer of Israel. They loved God on earth; they praised Him on earth; but in that country they will praise Him better and love Him more.

There we shall see JESUS, who is gone before us to that happy place; and there we shall behold the glory of the High God. We cannot see Him here, but we will love Him here; we must be now on earth, but we will often think on Heaven.

That happy land is our home; we are to be here but for a little while, and there for ever, even for ages of eternal years.